The Children of the Forest

ALSO BY ALAN L. SIMONS

MEMOIR

Eighteen Months – A Love Story Interrupted

FICTION

The Village of Little Comely-on-the-Marsh

The Village of Little Pletzl-on-the-Zump

The Village of Little Figgy-on-the-Duff

An Anthology of Witty & Oddball Village Stories

CHILDREN

Sweaty Cats and Baby Pigeons

The Incredible Adventures of Captain MacDuddyfunk in Cuggermuggerland

The Children of the Forest

(A historical fiction embellishment)

BARONEL BOOKS

Toronto, Canada.

The Children of the Forest

This edition is published by Baronel Books, Toronto, Canada.

Second edition, 2026.

Alan L. Simons asserts the moral right to be identified as the author of this work.

This work is a fictional embellishment.

Names, characters, places, and incidents are products of the author's vivid imagination and are not to be construed as real. Any resemblance to actual events, locales, or persons, living or dead, is entirely coincidental.

Library and Archives Canada Cataloguing in Publication information is available upon request.

ISBN: 978-1-7782137-8-6

(original trade paperback)

https://thechildrenoftheforest.com
thechildrenoftheforest@proton.me

To my dear family and friends, who continue to have the patience to put up with my unique sense of style.
Blessings to you!

AUTHOR'S NOTES

The Children of the Forest is a historical fiction embellishment. It is a folktale in the European tradition. Mystical. Kabbalistic. Klezmerising.

The story begins pre-WWII, weaving around the lives of its two primary characters: Zusa is ten, and Motke is nine, two Polish Jewish-born children who, one night, each lost both of their parents in a massive storm. During the ensuing years, they begin a lasting relationship.

Zusa, along with her friend Motke, encounter five complex and confounding Klezmorim characters, living with disabilities. The characters balance each other's strengths and weaknesses to form, as it were, one single, dynamic, and powerful voice.

The focus of the story also brings history to life for teens, increasing their knowledge in the field of social sciences and promoting the development of social-emotional skills, such as empathy and sensitivity.

Alan L. Simons, Toronto, Canada
January 2026.

I gratefully acknowledge JG for her support and constructive advice in the characterisations mentioned in this book.

I affirm that "The Children of the Forest" is very loosely based upon an unfinished work, "The Story of the Seven Beggars," written by Rabbi Nahman of Bratslav (1772-1810). Several quotes from various sources throughout this book are ascribed to Rabbi Nahman.

I am indebted to the late Professor Joseph Dan (1935-2022), who is regarded as one of the world's leading authorities on Jewish mysticism. Reading his book, "The Heart and the Fountain. An Anthology of Jewish Mystical Experience," gave me much to think about.

"Folklore, legends, myths and fairy tales have followed childhood through the ages."

-L. Frank Baum

-Part One-

1

Once upon a time, many years ago in the old historic town of Sanok, located on the banks of the San River below the Carpathian Mountains in south-eastern Poland, and the home of Shlomo Halberstam, the first Bobover Rebbe, lived two young children, Zusa, she was ten and Motke, he was nine.

They both lived on Sanowa Street and went to the same school. The children's parents were good friends with each other.

One evening when all the parents in Sanok had hugged their children and kissed them goodnight, tucked them into bed, and all the lights in the houses had been turned off, a ferocious rainstorm, the largest anyone had ever seen in their lives, with the San River rising at an enormous rate, caused many families to flee their homes.

In the torrential rain, many grandparents, parents, and their children were separated from each other. Among them were Zusa and Motke.

By chance, during the storm, Zusa and Motke tried to find their parents together.

"Mamme! Tate! Where are you? Where are you?" they both shouted at the top of their voices. But their parents didn't answer.

The rain continued for many days and nights until all the houses at the top of the hill and those in Sanok were swept away down the hill to the river's edge, where the houses broke into pieces and disappeared into the fast-moving water, never to be seen again.

Thankfully, Zusa and Motke saved themselves by holding hands and running up the hill to higher ground. They passed the Sanok Royal Palace, and fifteen minutes later, they entered the magical forest.

No one in Sanok had ever attempted to enter the forest before, for it was said the forest had no beginning or end. Besides, only scary people lived there. All of Sanok's children were told from the time they could walk never to play near the forest.

But for Zusa and Motke, it was the only place to run and shelter from the rainstorm. Amazingly, for some reason, the rain had not found its way into the forest.

"Perhaps our parents are also sheltering in the

forest," said Zusa.

"Mamme! Tate! Are you here?" shouted Zusa as loud as she could. But there was no reply, only the rustling of leaves in the trees.

"I'm frightened," said Motke. "It's so dark here. And look at the trees, they're looking at us. I want to go home! Please, let's go home. I'm getting hungry, and I'm cold."

Zusa stopped, looked around, and realized they were lost. She pointed ahead. "Okay, let's walk this way," she said, not wanting to frighten Motke even more than he was.

They walked for what seemed hours. Through the trees. Through the bushes and the shrubs. What they didn't realize was that the trees, bushes, and shrubs were helping them find their way by opening a path for them, as if to say, "Come along, we'll show you where to go. Don't be scared. We'll protect you!"

They were so tired and hungry. Suddenly, in front of them, they came across a beautiful tree. "Oh my," said Zusa. "Just look at all those different coloured leaves. I've never seen anything like this before. And look Motke, on every branch, there are different kinds of fruit."

"Wow!" said Motke. "Zusa, do you think we can eat any of them?" He reached up as far as he could and picked a fruit that looked like a combination of a plum and a mango.

"Be careful, Motke. It might be poisonous," said Zusa. Motke immediately threw the unusual-looking fruit onto the forest floor.

"Oh! I wish I could have an apple to eat," Motke said. Suddenly, to Zusa's and Motke's astonishment the unusual-looking fruit changed into a gorgeous large red apple.

It seemed as if the children had found a magical fruit tree. If they touched any fruit on the tree, and wished for their favourite type of fruit, the tree instantly produced what they asked for.

Zusa and Motke tasted one delicious fruit after another. But they liked the apples best.

Unexpectedly, from behind them, the trees shook. Zusa and Motke turned to see a very old lady with bright, sparkling pink hair watching them. She was dressed in some odd-looking green clothes, and she had a sack on her shoulder. Her green clothes matched the colour of the forest so well that she blended in with the surroundings.

The old lady slowly approached Zusa and Motke. Nervously, the children stood their ground.

She smiled at them. "Hello, how did you get here?" she asked.

“We’re lost and we’re looking for our parents who disappeared during Sanok’s violent rainstorm,” replied Zusa with tears in her eyes.

“What are your names?” asked the old lady. “I’m Zusa, and this is my friend Motke,” replied Zusa. “And what’s your name?”

The old lady smiled, “I have 195 names, equal to all the countries in the world.”

Motke looks at the old lady with amazement. “195 names? Why 195?”

The old lady sat down on the forest floor, tapped the fallen leaves around her, and beckoned the children to sit next to her.

“Every country is blessed with at least one

righteous person. I have always lived my life alone in this forest, yet through having each of the 195 names they become a personal attachment in my life. Their good deeds become my good deeds. It is as if all 195 names are like family to me. And I'm not alone."

The old lady smiled at them. "But you can call me Hanka."

She pointed to the thickness of the leaves of the trees above her that were gently rustling in response to her voice.

"You see, I feel their companionship. It is as if we are one."

Motke held Zusa's hand very tightly, while in his other hand, he offered the old lady his half-eaten apple.

"It tastes and smells so good. Hanka, would you like some?"

The old lady shook her head and explained she was born without the ability to be able to taste or smell food.

"Tell me Motke, what does it taste like?" she asked him.

"Well," said Motke, it tastes like swinging as high as I can in my park back home, with my Mamme and Tate pushing me on my swing."

"And what about for you, Zusa?"

Zusa smiled. "It's as if I'm sitting down in my garden under the big oak tree reading my favourite book about a princess who is saved by a prince."

"Hanka, can you please help us find our parents?" Zusa asked the old lady.

"No, I'm so sorry. I don't have the power to do that. But, if you look over my shoulders I can, through a magic window, show you an image of both of your parents. You can see them, but you cannot talk with them."

Zusa and Motke were so overcome with emotion upon seeing their parents that they burst into tears.

The old lady put her arms around the children, sighed, and said, "Come now, you must be hungry." She reached into her sack to produce a cooking pot, which she put down on the forest floor.

Immediately, the pot began to simmer and bubble with food. She put her hand again into her sack and produced bowls, knives, and forks, spoons, and bread to the delight of the very hungry children.

The old lady looked at Motke and then pointed to the magical fruit tree.

"Motke, over there. Can you see that strange-looking fruit that is green and brown?" Motke nodded.

"Can you please go and pick it for me? But be very careful not to accidentally cut it open. It's called a durian and it's the stinkiest fruit in the world. Bring it over here so that I can drop it into my magical pot. As soon as I do that, you will be able to eat it without a problem."

The children sat down, washed their hands at a nearby stream, and began to eat.

During their delicious meal, Zusa and Motke asked the old lady how it was possible she could make such a wonderful meal if she could not smell or taste the food.

"Zusa. Motke. Look at me!" The old lady produced from her sack some paints and brushes.

"Think of it this way. Here are the colours blue and yellow. If I mix them, what colour do I get?"

“Green!” replied the children.

“And now, red and blue?”

“Purple,” the children replied.

“Good! Now, if I took several colours of food growing in the forest, say for instance one black and one brown they would have no warm effect on me and would not produce a pleasant sensation. However, when I mix them, as you have done with the paints, such as blue with yellow and red with blue, it encourages me to cook and produce a good meal for you.”

After the meal had been finished, Hanka asked Zusa and Motke to hold hands, to close their eyes as she said a blessing. “May peace light upon you from the good Master, to whom all peace belongs.”

Later, as dusk turned into night, Zusa and Motke fell asleep on her shoulder. Hanka, the old lady, covered them with leaves and branches that magically turned into a warm blanket. Just before she disappeared into the forest, she blessed them that they would always remain protected and safe and eventually be united with their parents. “May you be able to lie down in peace at night and return to life the following day.”

"Always wear a smile. The gift of life will then be yours to give."

2

On the morning of the second day in the mystical forest, Zusa and Motke awoke to find the weather had changed for the worst. Even though the blanket Hanka had given them had kept them warm throughout the night, they were now cold and miserable and had very little suitable clothing to wear. Suddenly, out of the bushes an old man, with a long white beard and hair dangling over his ears, appeared.

He waved at them. He was wearing a large white coat, matching hoodie, and white boots that looked too large for him. He also carried a clarinet.

Zusa and Motke waved back at him.

The old man pointed to a spot behind them

where, suddenly, some warm clothing appeared. Amazingly, the clothes fitted perfectly.

Zusa and Motke approached the man to thank him, only to find he couldn't hear or speak, but he could lip-read.

He made them laugh so much. His fingers and hands moved unhurriedly as he taught them some simple sign language. Zusa and Motke were fast learners. They learned the signs for please, thank you, more, eat, drink, and that the man's name was Danek.

During the day, Danek shared his food with the children. He dug deep into his coat's many pockets and much to the surprise of Zusa and Motke, out came some potato dumplings called Silesian Kluski.

Danek was skilled at playing the clarinet. While they all danced together, he used the occasion to play some klezmer-style melodies. His tunes made the trees and bushes come alive as they swayed from side to side to the musical notes he expertly played. It was as if all the trees knew the music in advance. And their leaves, not to be left out, changed their colour from vibrant red to yellow to blue every time Danek played a new melody.

Through hand gestures, they asked the old man why he chose to play the clarinet. After all, he was deaf. How could he hear the music? He answered by telling them through sensation, touch, and vibrations from the forest floor. In addition, learning the clarinet had been good for his health, since it promoted good deportment and finger skills. All of which helped him take care of his body. He also explained to them that, as a young boy, he suffered from asthma and playing the clarinet had helped him breathe more efficiently.

By the end of the day, the children were exhausted from dancing, but not the old man. He continued to play his clarinet and dance around Zusa and Motke all through the night as they slept. His legs and his body didn't stop moving. He bent, jumped, turned, stretched, glided, and he knew all the movements of a dancer. It was as if he not only had an enchanted clarinet but also had superhuman powers.

The next morning, during breakfast, through hand gestures, they asked Danek to take them with him and help them find their parents.

"Danek, can you please help us find our parents?" Zusa asked him.

Sadly, Danek shook his head; for it was not in his power to do so.

"No, I'm so sorry. I don't have the power to do that. But, if you look over my shoulders I can, through a magic window, show you an image of both of your parents. You can see them, but you cannot talk with them."

Through his sign language, he asked Zusa and Motke to hold hands and close their eyes as he said a blessing just as Hanka had done, "May peace light upon you from the good Master, to whom all peace belongs." Just before he disappeared into the forest, he blessed them again that they would always remain protected and safe and eventually be united with their parents. "May you be able to lie down in peace at night and return to life the following day."

"Faith is not only in the heart, it should be put into words."

3

During the morning of their third day, they met a cheerful girl called Lejka. She was in a wheelchair. She asked them who they were and what they were doing in the forest.

Zusa and Motke explained their difficulty and asked her to help them find their way out of the forest. Lejka told them that she had never been out of the forest and didn't know the way, but she was so happy to make their acquaintance that they must come back to her home and have some milk and delicious rugelach she had recently made.

"I fill my rugelach with blackberry jam and pistachios," she said. "I do hope you enjoy it!"

The children were quite intrigued by Lejka. Not having any experience with a person in a wheelchair and without realizing it, they started to speak quite loudly to her. Lejka laughed and corrected them, pointing out that she might not be able to walk, but she can hear perfectly.

As they set out for her home the children wanted to push her wheelchair. "No thank you, I'm fine, really! I'm quite capable of moving on my own."

En route, she told Zusa and Motke that she was born with Spina Bifida, a birth defect of the spinal cord. "I have no use of my legs, so I must adapt. I refuse to accept my condition sitting down!" Zusa and Motke started to laugh.

"Lejka, do you realize you just made a funny joke?"

"Ooh! So I did, sitting down!" Lejka replied, with a huge smile on her face.

"Now sit over there on that old tree trunk and just watch me!"

Lejka showed the children some breathtaking wheelie stunts she could do while sitting in her wheelchair. They included spinning on one wheel around so much so that Zusa became giddy just watching her.

Lejka also balanced herself on the wheelchair's two back wheels and started hopping about as a kangaroo would, and jumping over some of the fallen tree trunks!

She looked at Zusa and Motke. "That's easy! I've just started to learn these tricks. You see, having a disability and being unable to walk should never let anything stop you from doing things you want to accomplish in life.

"I have a passion to succeed in what limited way I can. I dream of being an acrobat and having fun doing so. I know I have challenges ahead of me but look at what I have been able to achieve so far!"

"Oh, you are so amazing!" said Zusa. "Incredible!" added Motke.

"So, who wants some milk and rugelach?"

Zusa and Motke enjoyed their visit. Lejka was funny and lively and lived in a very cute little wooden house. Lejka dismissed the idea that people with disabilities are miserable and needy people.

"Lejka, can you please help us find our parents?" Zusa asked her.

Sadly, Lejka shook her head, for it was not in her power to do so.

"No, I'm so sorry. I don't have the power to do that. But, if you look over my shoulders I can, through a magic window, show you an image of both of your parents. You can see them, but you cannot talk with them."

Before Zusa and Motke said their goodbyes, Lejka filled their backpacks with homemade rugelach, strawberries, and apples, and two large servings of golabki, cabbage leaves stuffed with ground beef, rice, and cooked in tomato soup.

As they left, she asked Zusa and Motke to hold hands and close their eyes as she said a blessing just as Hanka and Danek had done, "May peace light upon you from the good Master, to whom all peace belongs." Just before Lejka disappeared into the forest, she blessed them again that they would always remain protected and safe and eventually be united with their parents. "May you be able to lie down in peace at night and return to life the following day."

4

Day four. After a restful night's sleep where the forest trees folded their branches over the children to keep them warm, Zusa and Motke awoke full of morning energy. They wondered what adventures the day would bring to them. They didn't have to wait very long.

"Hello! Who are you?" said a friendly voice from someplace in the bushes.

"I'm Zusa, and this is my friend Motke. Where are you? We can't see you."

The friendly voice laughed. "Well, I can't see you either!" From out of the bushes appeared an old man. He was dressed in a multitude of colours. His cloak around his shoulders was bright yellow. His hat was orange, and his trousers were green.

"Oh my!" said Zusa, looking at Motke, wondering who this person was. And why was he dressed this way?

The old man sensed the nervousness of the children. "Don't be afraid. My name is Zavel. As he approached Zusa and Motke they could see he was blind.

Motke bravely stepped forward. "We're not afraid of you!"

"Ah! But you believe only what your eyes can see. I suppose I must look different, and that must make me look frightening. Come closer. Let me see you!"

"But you're blind, how can you see us?" said Zusa.

"That's a very good question. Because I possess excellent tuned senses of hearing and touch and smell, much better than most people who are not blind," he replied.

Zusa and Motke were only an arm's length from the old man when he put up his right hand.

"Now, that's near enough! Let me see." He took a deep breath and smiled.

"Yes! You have visited Hanka, Danek and Lejka. Did you enjoy your days with them?"

"Oh yes, we did," replied Zusa. 'They were all so kind and generous towards us."

"And very helpful! We learned a lot from them," interrupted Motke.

"Tell me, what did you learn?" asked Zavel.

"Well, from Hanka, I learned all about colours, and by mixing them you can end up with warm colours or cold colours. And some make you happy, and others will make you sad."

Zavel turned to Zusa.

"And you, Zusa, what did you learn from Danek?"

Zusa smiled. "He taught us how to use sign language and how important music can be to bring people together."

"And Lejka?"

Zusa and Motke looked at each other. "You go first," said Zavel to Motke.

"Well, it was amazing! It was as if Lejka was an acrobat. She could do so many things in her wheelchair..."

Zusa interrupted Motke. "Motke, she *'is'* an acrobat! Just because she can't walk and she must spend all her awakening period in her wheelchair, doesn't mean she is unlike anyone else. She just must adapt to her life differently from ours. Oh my! She can do so much more than I can!" said Zusa with a sigh.

Zavel gestured to the children. "Come and sit down next to me."

"For you Zusa and your friend Motke, before you arrived in our forest you believed only what your eyes could see. Anyone who had a disability, as we have in this forest, frightened you because we look and act differently from your friends and family. And that's why your parents forbid you to play near our forest. They were trying to protect you from things they didn't understand. But as you have seen, we do live productive lives, don't you think so?"

The children nodded in agreement.

Zavel continued. "I have been blind from birth. Yet, like you I can socialize, I can tell apart the difference between day and night by hearing the sounds surrounding me.

"It is as if I have an invisible teacher, instructing me on the ways of the forest. When I step on a fallen twig from a tree or bush, I know from the sound what season it is. From touching the forest flowers, I know from the smell the differences of the fragrance and beauty you can see in each variety."

Motke was very confused. "I don't understand."

"Motke, let me explain it this way. Close your eyes. Just suppose you have never tasted chocolate ice cream and Zusa was trying her best to describe the taste to you. Unless you tasted it, how would you know what it would be like until you experienced it yourself?

"A blind person from birth does not know about connecting what the ice cream visually looks like with the taste of it. You are not blind, so you can experience connecting a visual sensation with what it looks like."

"And what about your dreams?" asked Zusa.

"That's a great question!" replied Zavel.

"Well, your dreams are full of visual images containing lighting and colours, but unlike your dreams, my dreams do not have visual pictures. I cannot dream in pictures as you can. You see, being blind from birth, I do not know about connecting visual sensations with external objects in the real world or relating them to what sighted people describe as vision.

"But my dreams, I am sure, are just as imaginative and intense as yours are," he added.

"You are our lerer, our teacher," said Zusa.

Zavel laughed. "But not invisible to you! Come now, let us eat. You must be hungry."

The children spent the whole day until late in the evening with Zavel. As the forest birds, the field voles, and squirrels bedded down for the night, Zavel bid the children goodnight. He asked Zusa and Motke to hold hands and close their eyes as he said a blessing just as Hanka, Danek and Lejka had done, "May peace light upon you from the good Master, to whom all peace belongs." Just before he disappeared into the forest, he blessed them again that they would always remain protected and safe and eventually be united with their parents. "May you be able to lie down in peace at night and return to life the following day."

"You are wherever your thoughts are; make sure your thoughts are where you want to be."

5

On the fifth day, Motke and Zusa cried out for someone to help them find a way out of the forest and reunite them with their loving parents. Unexpectedly, a lady appeared, but because she stuttered, they were unable to understand what she was saying. That was until she started to sing to them.

"Hello, my name is Sura, and I know how you can exit the forest by way of a mystical path leading out to a town called Skookum.

As the three walked together, Sura, in her singing voice, explained to the children that they must continue walking along the mystical path without looking back until they were well clear of the forest.

"You must take care, for at any point if either of you look back, you both will be returned to the original place you started from five days ago. It will be as if you have just entered the forest again without remembering anything of your previous experiences. You will return to a place that has no beginning or end. Do you understand what I'm saying to you?"

Zusa and Motke looked at each other and shook their heads in agreement. They were terrified.

"This is where I must say goodbye," Sura sang. "The branches of the trees will guide you along the path from now on. They have taken a liking to you. Do not be afraid. They will protect you. Remember what I said. Do not look back!"

They bid farewell to Sura as she blessed them, just as Hanka, Danek, Lejka and Zavel had done during the past four days and nights. She asked Zusa and Motke to hold hands and close their eyes. "May peace light upon you from the good Master, to whom all peace belongs." Just before she disappeared into the forest, she blessed them again that they would always remain protected and safe and eventually be united with their parents. "May you be able to lie down in peace at night and return to life the following day."

As Zusa and Motke walked along the path, they made a pact always to stay together and never forget how the five righteous forest grown-ups had helped them.

"Look over there, there's an opening!" Motke pointed to a place in the distance, where an amber glow emanated from between two pine tree saplings, beckoning them forward.

And as they approached the opening, every step they took increased their age until they arrived at the edge of the forest five years older.

They both took a deep breath, held hands, and looked at each other before stepping into another world they had no vision of.

For Zusa had become 15 years old and Motke 14 years old.

"If you won't be better tomorrow than you were today, then what do you need tomorrow for?"

-Part Two-

6

It was Farmers' Market Day in Skookum. A beautiful spring day. The sun was shining, the birds were chattering with each other, and the town was full of farmers and tradespeople selling their goods to the townsfolk. It was very well organized. Vegetables in one corner. Fruit in another. Cheese and dairy products had their location, and so did the market folk who were selling clothes, kitchen things, and furniture.

In addition, in the Town Square, musicians were entertaining the townsfolk, including a group of six Klezmers. Five of the Klezmers reminded Zusa and Motke of the five righteous forest grown-ups they had met during their forest adventures.

Since the children were hungry, to solicit money for food, they tried to copy the Klezmers' style of singing and performing. But the townsfolk either ignored them or made fun of them. Fortunately, one friendly Klezmer, Saul, took pity on Zusa and Motke and approached them.

"You'll never get anywhere with that act!" he said.

Saul was a kind, warm-hearted, and jolly person. "Come along. We'll set you straight." He invited Zusa and Motke to join the Klezmers for lunch. He introduced them to his friends.

"This is Anna. She's preparing our lunch. Anna plays the hammered dulcimer. Over there is Daniel, who plays the straw harmonica and clarinet. Leah is the one who's buying some cabbage. She plays the violin," he said pointing to Leah, who was in a wheelchair bargaining with the vegetable owner. "Sarah is under that apple tree practicing her singing. When she's not singing, she's playing her flute." Saul extended his hand towards Zusa and Motke. They could see he was blind.

"And I'm Saul, the leader of the group. And I play the trumpet." He turned to Deldor, who was suspiciously eyeing the children. "Oh yes! And this is our Deldor! She plays the accordion."

The Klezmers were an enthusiastic and welcoming group, except for Deldor, a young woman with a sour face and a whining voice. She criticized the children very cruelly and told Saul not to be a fool and waste time on these kids who don't have any talent and who, she said, were going to steal from them. Saul and the others ignored Deldor, but she remained a jealous bully who tried to undermine Motke and Zusa at every opportunity.

"Come, Anna is telling us it's time for lunch! We'll all sit over there on the grass." Saul pointed to a spot near the oak tree where Sarah was sitting.

Neither Zusa nor Motke was surprised at how easy it was for Saul to find his way around. For they had experienced far more mystical events during their time in the forest.

"This stew tastes delicious," said Zusa to Anna. "What's in it?"

"Oh! A bit of this. A bit of that," replied Anna. She looked directly at the children, smiled, and offered some more to them.

Zusa looked one by one at all the Klezmers. "Are you sure we haven't met before? There's something about all of you that is so familiar."

Sarah, for the first time, spoke up. Well, she didn't speak, she sang!

"A couple who is going to pick apples in the future is not the same couple who has picked apples in the past."

The Klezmers nodded in agreement but offered no explanation to Zusa and Motke.

Motke spoke up. "What exactly is a Klezmer?"

Saul replied. "The word Klezmer is as ancient as that old oak tree Sarah was sitting under. It comes about from two words. *klei,* meaning tools or instruments of, and *zemer* meaning melody. Joined together, these two words eventually became Klezmer, meaning musicians. And that is what we are. We are Klezmers!"

"Klezmer groups like ours perform all over the

country. At weddings, in guesthouses, and sometimes for kings and queens, and even as it is today, during Skookum's weekly Farmer's Market," said Daniel.

Leah turned towards Zusa. "So, tell me, can you sing? What musical instrument can you play?"

Zusa turned bright red. "Sorry, I can't play any instrument, and as far as my singing..."

"Oh, don't worry," said Anna.

"But I do remember a poem my grandmother always used to sing to me," said Zusa. "Shall I try singing it to you now?"

All the Klezmers nodded their heads in agreement:

> *"Ikh bin a royz fun shrun, a lilye fun di valiz.*
> *Vi a lilye tsvishn derner, azoy iz meyn libe tsvishn di tekhter.*
> *Vi der epl boym tsvishn di beymer fun di holts, azoy iz meyn libe tsvishn di kinder.*
> *Ikh gezesn aunter di shotn mit groys freyd, aun di frukht iz zis tsu meyn geshmak."*

Zusa stopped singing and started to cry. "I miss my parents so much. I miss my family. Whatever happened to them?"

Anna came over to Zusa and put her arm around her shoulder.

"I shall translate your beautiful words for you. They are taken from the Songs of Solomon:"

> *"I am a rose of Sharon, a lily of the valleys.*
> *As a lily among thorns, so is my love among the daughters.*

As the apple tree among the trees of the wood,
so is my love among the children.
I sat down under the shadow with great
delight, and the fruit was sweet to my taste."

Motke quietly walked over to join his friend Zusa and held her hand.

"Yes, it is as if we no longer have parents. But we still have hopes and dreams of seeing them again, sometime, somewhere."

Leah held Zusa's other hand. "Zusa, there's a very old saying. Many waters cannot quench love, neither can the floods drown it. Perhaps there will be a time when you will be reunited with your parents. In the meantime..."

"In the meantime, we are your family," interrupted Saul. "Now, before all the sleeping accommodations this evening in Skookum become booked, I think we should find a place for our new friends."

"Come along," said Anna. "I know the very place. Leave everything to me."

"The man who acts humble in order to win praise is guilty of the lowest form of pride."

7

When morning came, Zusa and Motke had arranged to meet the Klezmers in Skookum's Town Square at 10 o'clock. But not before they had decided to get up as early as possible to explore Skookum, which was far bigger than Sanok, where they had lived for many years before the big storm.

As they walked around Skookum, they were surprised to find that many things were like those in Sanok. The market square, the town hall, and the parks all looked so much like Sanok.

"I bet Skookum isn't as famous as Sanok," said Motke to Zusa. "I bet it doesn't have a Royal Castle. I bet it doesn't have a Rebbe Shlomo Halberstam, the first Bobover Rebbe, I bet it doesn't have . . ."

"Enough of I bet it doesn't have," interrupted Zusa. "Yes, I know you have happy memories of Sanok and so do I, and how something like this could happen to us. It's as if we walked into a huge cave and disappeared. But we survived, Motke. We survived thanks to the five wonderful, righteous forest grown-ups. Oh! I do miss them."

"Ah, there you are. We were wondering where you got to!" It was Sarah. 'I've been looking all over for you. Come on now, quickly, it's time for your first day as a Klezmer. You have lots to learn."

Saul and the other Klezmers were waiting for them in the Town Square.

Saul greeted them with a big smile.

"You're just in time! We've all discussed the best way to introduce you into the group, and we've decided that for the next two days you should just observe us and see how we perform for our audience."

All the Klezmers agreed, except for Deldor.

"Who are these children? They don't deserve our help. Let them go and earn money for themselves. We're not their parents!"

Deldor walked right up to Zusa and Motke, gave them an evil look, and said, "Go away! We don't want you here! Go back to where you came from! You're not like us. You're different. Just look at the strange clothes you're wearing. And the way you speak, with your strange accent, you're not one of us! Go away!"

The other Klezmers were shocked at Deldor's behaviour. But they said nothing. It was left to Zusa to have the last word. She raised her hand in a non-aggressive way toward the Klezmers. "It's okay, I will handle this myself!"

"Deldor," she started to say, maintaining eye contact with Deldor, while her voice was full of composure. "I respect you, but I don't understand why you are so aggressive towards us. Are you frightened of us? Why are you bullying us? Have we offended you in some way? Is it because you believe we are different from you? Please explain. We want to solve the problem you have with us so that we can all find a way to move forward. Deldor, please explain."

No one had ever spoken to Deldor in this way before. She didn't know what to say. She thought all the other Klezmers were so negative towards her. They were always putting her down and making fun of her.

Zusa repeated her comment. "Deldor, please explain." Zusa confidently stood in silence, facing Deldor, waiting for a response. But none came. Deldor just walked away.

Zusa was very proud of herself. She had used her right to express herself, honestly and without anger. She had stood up to a bully but now it was time for her to also walk away.

"Right now! That's over with," said Saul with a sigh of relief. "It's time for us to start playing to the people of Skookum. Zusa and Motke, I want you to stand over there, at the far end of the square, and watch people's reactions to us and the various songs we will play. Here's the list of our songs. Your work will be to ask people what they liked. Just tick the list off from 1 to 10, with 10 being their most favourable. You both have a very important job to do. We must know what songs they like."

Zusa and Motke nodded their heads in

agreement. They knew they could easily follow Saul's instructions.

"Good! Off you go then!" Saul had a big smile on his face. It was a smile of confidence. All the Klezmers were smiling, except for Deldor.

8

The day went by very fast for Zusa and Motke. Besides receiving many answers from the people listening to the music, they also had time to dance to the melodies, a fact that didn't go unnoticed by the Klezmers.

Zusa and Motke travelled with the Klezmers from town to town, from village to village, performing as members of the group to many important people, such as kings and queens, prime ministers, and mayors. But wherever they went, they never stopped asking the townsfolk if they knew of their parents, much to the annoyance of Deldor, who continued telling the other Klezmers that someday they would regret accepting Zusa and Motke into the group. Fortunately, all the other Klezmers closed their ears to Deldor's continual bullying.

As time went by, Motke became the announcer, explaining to the audience, in detail, the history of the songs and the musical instruments played by each Klezmer member. And Zusa became a gifted singer, poetry reader, and a great mystical storyteller. Her reputation grew mostly from her storytelling.

Every day, after the Klezmers had performed, her storytelling became part of the Klezmers' performance. She drew great crowds.

The stories she would tell were based on what she remembered as a young girl, told to her by her grandmother.

One story received much attention from the audience.

Zusa would always start by saying, "Once upon a time, long ago," and a hush would immediately fall upon the audience.

"Once upon a time, long ago, in a faraway land, lived a young girl who spent many hours studying at her religious school. One day, on arriving home, she found three holy men in her kitchen talking with her father.

'Come here daughter, I want you to meet our guests. They will be staying overnight. They want to bless you,' said her father.

The young girl approached them but suddenly

stopped and returned to her father's side.

'No father,' she said, 'I have been taught in my school that if one has not said their prayers, nor washed their hands, they cannot bless me.'

The holy men were shocked and admitted they had been too busy visiting needy families, and there was no one to assist them.

'How did you know this?' asked one of the holy men.

The young girl replied. 'I knew immediately I saw you, from your appearance. Your clothes are smelly, your beards still have food in them, and your sandals are dusty. You would not have said the prayers in that condition. Nor would you have sat down in our kitchen and accepted a cup of tea and a meal from my father.'

The three holy men were not used to being spoken to in this way. Yet, they sat at the table, after washing their hands, sipped on the tea, and ate the cake in front of them. Sadly, one of the men, whose hands were still dirty, said the blessing before washing.

The young girl was very angry. 'I don't believe you are holy. If you are, you would not have said the blessing with dirty hands!'

Her father was very embarrassed. He started to apologize to the three men.

His daughter stopped him. 'Father, in my school we are taught that anyone who says the blessing with dirty hands deserves to die!

'It is said in Exodus 30:20: *When they go into the tent of meeting, they shall wash with water, that they not die!*'

The three holy men sat in silence.

'In school, we learn that whoever does not wash

their hands before the blessing and appears before the King with dirty hands, is punishable by death. In our house, my dear father is the King.' The daughter continued. 'Since you are supposed to be so wise, why do you not follow our religious instructions? Do you not know that dirt and filth are part of the evil one? Do you not know that by washing our hands before a blessing makes us clean in the Holy One's eyes?'

The three holy men sat there, unable to speak. Finally, one of the men stood up and said, 'Child, where is your mother?'

The young girl looked at the holy man and then walked over to her father and held his hand.

'Father, shall I tell this man about my mother?'

Her father whispered in her ear, 'My daughter, have you decided who these three men are?'

'Yes, I have,' she whispered back, 'and I have found all three absent in their holy knowledge.'

The daughter returned to face the three holy men and said to them: 'You asked about my mother. She recently departed from this world to join her beloved righteous sisters, Sarah, Rebecca, Rachel, and Leah. May all their souls be bound up in the bond of eternal life.'

The holy men silently sat in their chairs and continued sipping their tea.

The daughter responded to their silence. 'Now I know I was correct about you. You come into my father's house unclean, without any knowledge of our traditions, without knowing that when someone has died, it is our custom to ask the name of the departed and say, *May their memory be for a blessing*. You call yourself holy men? And now I shall not tell you my mother's name, for we do not want a blessing from strangers who are not pure.'

Upon hearing those words, the three holy men arose from where they were sitting and said their goodbyes to the father. One of them turned to the daughter and said to her: 'You are not from this world,' to which her father responded to him that my daughter's world is purer than yours."

At the end of Zusa's storytelling, there were always questions from both the grown-ups and the teens. However, one question always repeated itself: Who were the three holy men? Zusa explained it this way: She said they were evil creatures from the dark side, dressed in disguise as holy men, and sent by Satan to test the honour and religious knowledge of the father and his daughter.

Throughout the country, in the towns and villages, in the hills and mountain areas, with strange sounding names such as Łańcut, Krosno, Humniska, Haczów, and Rzeszów and in the great palaces, the Klezmers, Zusa, and Motke all became loved for their music and storytelling.

And, as in their past travels, Zusa and Motke never stopped asking the townsfolk if they had known their parents. None of them did.

It was in Łańcut that Zusa and Motke felt a special attraction. With its castle in the centre of the town, they both felt it was the nearest thing to what they remembered in their childhood. But neither of them knew the reason why. It was just an inner feeling. It stimulated their curiosity and brought back memories of Sanok, their parents and grandparents.

"I have a feeling I have been here before," Zusa said to Motke.

"Yes, I do also, but it's just a feeling, nothing more than that!" replied Motke.

Zusa sighed. "It's times like these more than ever that I start remembering my mamme and tate. Oh, Motke, do you ever wonder what happened to your parents? Do you ever wonder if they are still alive?"

"Yes, all the time," replied Motke. "Zusa, perhaps it's time, after all these years, that we return to Sanok. I'm sure there must be some of our childhood friends still living there. Tell me, have you ever wondered why the Klezmers have never performed in Sanok?

"Zusa, the Klezmers, do you still believe we have met them before, in another place? Where though? I just can't imagine."

Zusa just shrugged her shoulders. It was also a mystery to her.

"Zusa! Motke!" It was Saul and Sarah, waving and briskly walking towards them with huge smiles.

"We have some exciting news to tell you! Guess what! No, don't guess, I'll tell you right now!" said Saul. "We have been invited to play at Łańcut's Annual Music Festival. What an honour! Can you just imagine? Us Klezmers!"

"And that's not all!" He was interrupted by Sarah.

"You, Zusa, have been asked to perform one of your mystical stories to a very distinguished audience in the famous Łańcut Synagogue. And Motke, you are to talk about the history of Klezmer at the Łańcut Castle just before we play there."

Their good news brought an immediate ending to the thoughts Zusa and Motke had of returning home to Sanok.

"Get into the habit of singing a tune. It will give you new life and fill you with joy. Get into the habit of dancing. It will displace depression and dispel hardship."

9

Zusa was the first to go on stage to a packed audience at the famous Łańcut Synagogue. Now a museum, it was one of the most valuable monuments of Jewish religious architecture in the land. It was a very fearful experience for her.

The night before she had had a dream of being on stage surrounded in a circle by a group of ten men. The men were not threatening her, and she didn't feel frightened. They all had warm smiles on their faces as if to say to her, 'Welcome Zusa, we have been waiting a long time for you.'

All ten men had grey beards with long strands of braided or unbraided hair hanging down in front of their ears and they were dressed in similar strange clothes. They wore very large round hats made of fur. Their black frock coats were long and made of silk and they were wearing high white socks with their pants tucked in them.

One of the men started to hum a melody that sounded familiar to Zusa and then all the other men put their arms around each other's shoulders and started to hum as well as dance around her in a circle.

At no time did Zusa feel threatened, but her arms tingled with goosebumps!

She tried to speak to the men, but nothing came out of her mouth.

The men's movements became more dramatic as they danced and sang around her. She was getting light-headed watching them as they moved faster, always singing the same unusual words, always smiling at her, and always looking directly into her eyes.

Zusa woke up the next morning, sweat dripping from her forehead. Who were these men? Why ten men? What was the melody they were singing? Why were they dressed so strangely? Why were they continually smiling at her? And why did the vivid dream occur the night before her first performance at the famous Łańcut Synagogue?

It was not just her first performance. But it was the first time the synagogue had been used for any non-religious event, an important point the Stage Manager told Zusa.

"Now a museum, the synagogue was erected in

1761 with the support of Prince Augustyn Dąbrowski. This evening in the audience, there in the front row, are several of his descendants."

As Zusa walked onto the stage, a hush took over the audience. Out of respect, Zusa curtsied to the Dąbrowski family, took a deep breath, and started to speak.

"Once upon a time, long ago, an extraordinarily rich man with his servant, travelled to a foreign land to seek out business. He had with him large sums of money, gold, and diamonds. His wife, who was pregnant, and their children remained at home.

"As soon as he arrived in the foreign land he died and his servant, claiming to be his son, not his servant, took ownership of all his money, gold, and diamonds.

"In the meantime, his widowed pregnant wife gave birth to a son. When the boy grew up, he found out about the lying servant and in time also his address, and he decided to seek legal advice on how to get back his inheritance.

"The former servant by now had managed to marry into a family of great wealth and political power. This frightened the cheated son, who was afraid his mother and siblings would be harmed.

"It so happened that a rabbi, known for his good wisdom, was passing the unhappy son's house and stopped by for a glass of water.

"Out of respect, the son's mother offered him something to eat. But he refused to touch the food until he revealed the real reason he had stopped by the house. For he had heard of the son's story and wished to help him.

"The rabbi recommended that the son bring the matter directly to a worthy prince, known for his devotion and kindness to his people and respect for the Bible.

"He did, and the prince at once sent for the rabbi to decide on the case.

"With the approval of the prince, the rabbi first instructed the former servant to draw blood into a bowl where a bone from the dead father had been placed, to see if any of the blood would be absorbed by the bone. It did not!

"Thereafter, the son was instructed to do the same using another bowl. The father's bone willingly absorbed the blood, proving the blood and the bone were of the same body.

"The rabbi presented his findings to the prince who ordered that all the money in the possession of the former servant should be returned to the real heir."

Zusa paused, looked at the audience, and said: "Some of you honourable people here today might regard my mystical story as nothing more than a folktale. I do not."

She added: "Is it not in Deuteronomy 4:40 that it is written:

> *'So you shall keep His statutes and His commandments which I am giving you today, that it may go well with you and with your children after you, and that you may live long on the land which the Lord your God is giving you for all time."*

There was much silence in the synagogue as Zusa continued. "Amongst you, you have the children's children of that worthy prince who presided over the decision to return the inheritance to the rightful owner. Those children are sitting below me in the front row."

Zusa quietly walked off the stage, and for thirty seconds a silence prevailed throughout the hall. No one in the audience had experienced such an event before. They were at a loss for words. Who was this girl, a stranger, still in her teens, who not only could express herself with the poise of an adult much older than her years, but knew so much about Łańcut's history and their famous family?

It might have been different if only Zusa knew who she was, and why she told a story she had no knowledge of. It was as if another soul had planted the words in her mouth. Her task was to simply tell it.

"I think you had better come and sit down," said the Stage Manager. "You look very pale. I will bring you a glass of water. I will just be a minute."

While waiting, Zusa looked up and saw images of the ten men from her dream the night before looking down at her. One of them came forward, smiled, nodded and said, "Sheynem dank!" With that, all the ten men vanished.

"You're shivering," said the Stage Manager. "Are you okay?"

Zusa explained she had just seen the images of ten men, and one of the men had said words she didn't understand.

"Sheynem dank," he said.

The Stage Manager smiled softly. "Zusa, this is an old building, with lots of memories in its stones. Some of these memories are good and some...well, it was a synagogue at one time with a splendid vibrant congregation, most of whom were ..."

The Stage Manager's voice faded. "Sheynem dank means, thank you very much!"

10

By the time Zusa had returned to join her friends, news about her speech had reached them. It was the talk of the town. But, on all the townsfolk's lips, one curious question was asked about her. Who was this young girl and where did she come from? Some people were frightened at Zusa's ability to speak outright on some mystical and religious experiences, and some people were just mystified as to how knowledgeable she was.

One thing was for sure. Her appearance helped Motke's and the Klezmers' concert later in the day at the Łańcut Castle. For their act had now become a sell-out! No more tickets were available. The townsfolk knew Zusa was part of the group and expected something similar from Motke and the Klezmers. They weren't to be disappointed, but not in the way they expected.

Łańcut Castle is one of the great residences in the country. Over many centuries the castle was visited by kings and queens, princes and princesses, dukes and duchesses, and the occasional politician. So, it was a real honour to be invited to play there. It was also the first time a Klezmer group was to perform on stage.

Curtain up! Motke was upstage. The Klezmers were behind him. They were all facing the audience who respectfully applauded them.

"Good evening, ladies and gentlemen. My name is Motke and behind me are the Klezmers." Another polite applause from the audience.

With that, Motke was prepared! He had lost all his nervousness, and he introduced, one by one, all the members of the Klezmer group. "Anna plays the hammered dulcimer. Daniel plays the clarinet and straw harmonica. Leah is our violinist. This is our charming singer, Sarah. Deldor is our accordionist, and finally, but not least... our Klezmer leader Saul, plays the trumpet."

After the introduction, Motke explained the various musical instruments and their history. He also said, with a smile, he had a story to tell.

The audience became excited. They wondered if the story would be like the story Zusa had told. It wasn't!

Motke cleared his throat. He began:

"There was a young boy who had nine siblings. All of them were older. He was the youngest. His name was Leizer and he was seven years of age. It was his birthday party. He always loved his birthdays. There were always lots of sweets and fresh fruit, a chocolate birthday cake, and presents.

"Can you remember your birthday parties when your mother and father, your grandparents, your aunts and uncles, and your siblings joined in singing happy birthday to you?

"Do you remember how they all clapped their hands after you blew all the lit candles out that were dripping down on your birthday cake? And then, one of your uncles would start to sing. Tell me, how does it go? How does it go?"

And with that, the Klezmers started to play the famous birthday song *Sto lat.*

Sto lat, sto lat,
Niech żyje, żyje nam.
Sto lat, sto lat,
Niech żyje, żyje nam,
Jeszcze raz, jeszcze raz, niech żyje, żyje nam,
Niech żyje nam!

A hundred years, a hundred years,
May she live for us.
A hundred years, a hundred years,
May she live for us.
Once again, once again, may she live, live for us,
May she live for us!

The audience went wild with pleasure and

started to accompany the Klezmers by singing as loudly as they could all the words of the birthday song.

Motke shouted above the noise of the audience. “Is it someone’s birthday here today?” And it was! Many birthdays! Every time somebody stood up and raised their hand, the audience applauded, and they once more started to sing the birthday song, just for the person.

The Klezmers were very shrewd. Every time it was somebody’s birthday, a different Klezmer would take the lead, come to the front of the stage, and play solo for the first few bars of the music. In that way, the audience heard and began to appreciate Klezmer’s musical ability. And this continued throughout the day, with Klezmer songs, and at the end of their final song, the audience gave them enough bravo and encore to last them until the next day! It was truly an event to remember. Even Deldor was smiling.

From Łańcut, as their reputation grew, Zusa and Motke, together with the Klezmers, toured many towns, including Krosno, Rzeszów, and Brzozów. Also the villages of Humniska, Haczów, and Wydrna. However, they never visited Sanok, where, as children, they had lived with their parents.

It was in the town of Brzozów that Zusa and Motke met a rabbi by chance, the only Jew left living in the town. He had a story to tell them:

“According to my religion, tradition dictates that there are not just 10 commandments but a total of 613.

These commandments are separated into positive commandments, commands to perform certain actions, of which there are 248, and negative commandments, those which we should abstain from certain actions, of which there are 365.

"Now, for the positive commandments, if you add together 2+4+8, you arrive at a total of 14. By adding 1+4, you arrive at the number of 5."

Zusa and Motke were all ears.

The rabbi continued.

"Now, shall we look at the negative commandments? There are 365. Add 3+6+5 and one arrives at the number..."

"14!" interrupted Motke. "And 1+4 also equals 5," he said with a smile.

"Good!" responded the rabbi. "In truth, of course, there is no limit, no number that can be put on the amount of positive and negative commandments, but let us, for one minute, believe you can."

Zusa and Motke nodded, and the rabbi grinned.

"Motke, you have shown us that although the number of commandments between each other differ, they both in the end not only add up together to 10, but they are equally the same."

The rabbi paused.

"I wonder why that is. Perhaps it's like the battle between good and evil. Sometimes the number of positive deeds you perform during your life is less than those that are negative deeds. Surely, it is not the number that counts. It's the difference between quality over quantity. In this situation you are at least starting on an equal footing. The next stage is up to you.

"Judaism says, as it has been written, 'We do not

need the Almighty's salvation to overwhelm the evil within us. It is an endless fight but to become a better person we must believe that our work is to do it ourselves.'"

The rabbi looked directly at Zusa and Motke. "You do understand, don't you? Your lives have been intermingled since you were young children. From the time you entered that forest on a rainy night, you have supported each other wisely. Yet, the areas of good and evil have always intermingled, and as you move forward it will be your duty to separate them.

"For you, the future has been written. Only you do not know what's to come."

Both Zusa and Motke were shaken by the rabbi's knowledge of their past. Not even their Klezmer friends knew of it, for they had never spoken to them about it during the years they had known them.

"I say to you," said the rabbi, "your lives so far have been good. Now, as you become well-known and you bask in the goodness of people, times will change. Up to now you have been sitting in paradise in a world where evil has not encroached. But the darker side is waiting, it is observing your every movement and waiting for the opportunity to come into your life. I warn you, take heed."

With that the rabbi disappeared, never to be seen again.

11

As the months went by Zusa and Motke, who had become celebrities in their own right, travelled with the Klezmers from town to town, from village to village, They never stopped looking for their parents, always asking if anyone knew their mother and father.

With the Klezmers, they performed throughout the country in front of many people, including royalty, singing, clowning, dancing, and miming. By now they had learned all areas of the theatre.

Yet, throughout these times Deldor never stopped trying to make Zusa and Motke look foolish by humiliating them. She spread bad rumours about their background, the way they spoke, their religion, and always behind their backs, never in front of them, or in front of the other Klezmers. For she has become a nasty, cruel bully from the dark side and one that the Rabbi of Brzozów told Zusa and Motke to watch out for.

"Up to now, you have been sitting in paradise, in a world where evil has not encroached. But the darker side is waiting, observing your every movement and waiting for the opportunity to come into your life. Take heed," he had said to them.

Seasons turned into years, and Zusa and Motke fell in love with each other. All the Klezmers, except for Deldor, suggested that sooner or later a wedding might be in order, and they wanted very much to make the wedding for them.

Zusa and Motke were beside themselves, what a wonderful surprise! Their friends, the Klezmers were family. All the Klezmers wanted to show Zusa and Motke how much they meant to them.

"Thank you so much," said Zusa. "Motke and I agree, but only if the wedding service takes place in our forest, where many years ago, we were saved by the five righteous forest grown-ups who befriended us."

"We are the children of the forest, and we owe our debt of gratitude to those who sheltered us during that time," said Zusa.

"And there's something else," said Motke. "We have never performed in the town where we were born, the town of Sanok. Why not? What has stopped us? Why have you purposely avoided entertaining the people of Sanok? Is there something horrible about the town? We love you all dearly, but now it is about time you told us your objection. And here's another question. All of you, except for Deldor, look very familiar to us. Are you related to our five righteous forest grown-ups?"

All the Klezmers looked at each other in silence. There were no longer the familiar smiles on any of their faces.

Saul stepped forward. "So many questions, all of them will lead to many more questions from you." Saul turned towards his Klezmer friends. "Perhaps I shall start and Sarah, Daniel, Leah, and Anna will join in to help me."

Saul took a deep breath. "Yes, Sanok. I'm sure it is now a beautiful town with decent people living there. But for us, it also has terrifying memories that go back many years ago. We still have nightmares from our experiences. And those memories are not ones we want to share with you, at least not yet, no, not yet. Perhaps never!"

It was Anna who continued. "Zusa. Motke. There's a saying, Where there is love, it never feels crowded. From the time we first saw you, we have seen you both grow and mature into beautiful and compassionate adults. We love you very much. You are part of our family." Anna had tears in her eyes. "You are the children none of us could have."

It was Leah's turn. "I'm sure all your questions will be answered in their own time. We promise you that. At your age, we know you want to have instant answers to your questions. Sometimes though, it's not possible, and this is one of those moments. Entering your forest will bring back hateful memories for us that we have tried to conceal from others for many years. Please try to understand."

Daniel stepped forward. He was the quietest of the Klezmer group. "Yes, for us our memories of what we have experienced are like great mountains that suddenly dip into hateful depths of the earth."

All five Klezmers nodded in agreement.

Daniel looked at Zusa and Motke. "These memories are today for many people just children's play words. They use our memories as if they are insignificant. Many deny them. They use our memories as if they are public property. Do not judge Deldor by her words and actions towards you. She conceals a darkness that goes far beyond any words you will recognize."

Zusa looked at Motke, stretched her open arms towards the Klezmers, and smiled. "Remember, many waters are not able to quench love, and rivers do not overpower it!"

The five Klezmers, Zusa, and Motke hugged each other. Deldor was nowhere to be seen.

12

The Klezmers, because of their history, were clear about entering the forest. They were worried about their reactions to a world they had left many years ago, but strangely, they were more concerned for Deldor. This puzzled Zusa and Motke. After all, Deldor had acted like a bully towards them and nothing Zusa or Motke did to extend a friendship to her helped. Why were the Klezmers defending Deldor?

Over the past years, Deldor had, at every step, verbally

abused Zusa and Motke. Yet, the five other Klezmers, and certainly not in front of them, had said nothing to her. Why not? What were the Klezmers hiding? Should Zusa and Motke be on their guard?

It was in the town of Brzozów, in the Market Square, that Zusa felt uncomfortable. She couldn't explain it. "Motke, there's something about this place where we're sitting that's making me nervous," she said, while they drank coffee and shared a pancake made with banana, roasted almonds, and caramel sauce.

Motke shrugged his shoulders. He hadn't sensed anything special about the town, other than the many wooden churches for which Brzozów was known. But there again, Zusa had always been the one to experience the unusual. This was no exception.

After Brzozów the next town the Klezmers, Zusa, and Motke visited was Krosno, where they appeared at the annual Karpackie Klimaty Festival. The audience loved them all, and in appreciation, the city gave each of them a gift of glassware from the famous Krosno Glass Heritage Centre.

Months went by as the Klezmers, Zusa, and Motke continued to increase their popularity, entertaining people in many towns and villages. It was in Haczów, after a concert at the village's Cultural and Leisure Centre, Zusa and Motke, who during dinner, finally stood their ground.

"My dear friends," said Zusa as she looked, one by one, at Saul, Anna, Leah, Daniel, Sarah, and Deldor. "You are our family. We love you very much and we know you love us. Motke and I will always remember the time many years ago in Skookum when you invited us to join you. And now look at us. We have all become famous! We have performed in front of nobility and the aristocracy, in front of townspeople, labourers, and clergy in many places."

All the Klezmers nodded their heads in agreement.

"But, as you know, we have never performed in the place where Motke and I were born, the town of Sanok. The place where our parents vanished, the place where our homes disappeared into the river during a violent storm."

None of the Klezmers had smiles on their faces. Saul raised his hand.

"Saul, please don't interrupt me. I promise you, you will have time to talk after I finish."

Zusa continued.

"Motke and I have told you we want to be married in our forest and invite, as special guests, the five wonderful righteous forest grown-ups who saved us and helped us find all of you. The forest still holds a special affection for us. As children, we learned that even if you are physically challenged, we are all equal in different ways."

Zusa looked at Motke for encouragement. He smiled lovingly at her.

"We want you to be present at our wedding. It

would not be the same without you. And we want to introduce you to our five forest friends, those of them who live in our forest. For we are the children of the forest."

Zusa took a deep breath.

"Motke and I have decided that after our wedding, we will be returning to Sanok to find out more about our past and to discover what happened to our parents. We would also be happy if all of you, including Deldor, accompany us to Sanok."

It was Motke's turn to say something.

"Yes, we want you with us at our wedding. You are the only family we know we have."

Zusa turned towards Motke and hugged him. She had tears in her eyes as she turned to face the Klezmers.

"Last night I had a dream. I was looking up at a tall hill. It reached the top of the sky. Two elderly people were standing right at the top while I was at the bottom. I couldn't climb up the hill because it was straight like a wall. I was shocked at seeing the two elderly people, for they looked like my parents. I shouted up at them, 'How can you, who are old, climb a wall, whereas I am young and cannot do so?' The man replied to me. 'Don't you know that I descend and ascend the hill to help you perform good deeds?'

"In my dream, I became frightened and started to cry. Who was this man who looked like my father? He told me not to be frightened of him, for this was his mission, to watch over me.

"I then saw by his side a long ladder reaching from the earth to the sky. But from the earth the ladder only had three rungs on it, all of which were separated from each other by one metre. The old man said he had been permitted to help me climb the three rungs, but not until I had decided to visit Sanok. Then he disappeared. I couldn't stop crying.

"I looked up to the top of the ladder and saw a beautiful woman standing there. The sun's beams were shining on her face. She was smiling as she was looking down at me. She asked me why I had been crying. 'Zusa, I am here to help you,' she said.

"By some miracle, she reached down with her right hand and brought me up the hill to be at her side. I realized then she was the image of my mother. I couldn't stop crying, and I asked her to help me persuade the Klezmers to join us at our forest wedding ceremony and also return to Sanok. She said nobody could help me but myself.

"Then the man appeared again as he did the first time on top of the hill. He took hold of my left hand and said to me that he would take me to a garden full of apple trees. We entered the garden. A river flowed at our feet, not unlike the one I remembered when I was young, living in Sanok. Birds hovered above the water's edge. Turtle doves, swallows, and sparrows were plentiful.

"As he took me further into the garden, I saw a house that I recognized as the one I had lived in on Sanowa Street. On the side of the house, there was a ladder leaning against a window, the window of my parents' bedroom. I turned around to speak to the man, but he was nowhere to be seen. I climbed the ladder and entered my parents' bedroom. My parents were sitting on a bench, looking at me. I was shaking, and my legs gave way. I fell to the ground between my parents. My father held out his hand and helped me get up. He looked at me, smiled, and gently said he was giving me the strength and courage to persuade my Klezmer friends to attend our forest wedding ceremony. My mother spoke: 'Zusa, do you like this place?' I asked my mother if this was heaven. She shook her head, smiled at me, and said I was still too young and that I had much to learn before my days came to an end.

"My father looked directly into my eyes. He said: 'Child, go in peace and remember the images you have seen and experienced. Go now and return to your friends. They are all waiting for you.'"

Deldor was the first to approach Zusa. She walked slowly towards her, but not as the bully she had been. For now, her head was down, her shoulders slouched, and she was trembling.

"Please forgive me. I have intimidated you and Motke. It wasn't my wish to upset you. I was frightened my Klezmer friends would love you more than they love me."

Deldor looked at Zusa. "Who are you? You came into our world from a world we wanted to forget. Our world was one of persecution, of hatred, of criminals and fanatics, and you, from where you came, brought us great joy and love. How is this so?

"You tell us that we remind you of the five

righteous forest grown-ups that helped you come to us. Are we that similar to them? As young children, during a spring day, we also ran into your forest, but not because of the storm you experienced. We were being chased by men in uniform who wanted to kill us. Our storm contained the blackest, evil storm that you have no concept of, or that we wish upon you."

All the Klezmers joined Deldor. "Yes, Zusa and Motke, we are also from the town of Sanok. "Unlike you and Motke, we have no memory of what happened to us in your forest. All we remember is that as soon as we entered the forest, during that spring day, we were whisked by ghostlike creatures to Skookum, the town where we first met you. None of us has supernatural abilities, as you seem to have. We were just simple, ordinary children running from death."

Deldor continued: "Zusa, are you one of the supernatural beings who protected us when we were children? But now, have you entered our world here to persuade us to return to your forest and to Sanok in payment for saving our lives?

"Unlike you, we don't have a memory of what happened to us while we were in your forest. It is as if time did not exist. We ran into the forest as children, fearful that if we didn't, we were going to be killed and then, mystically, we arrived in Skookum as grown-ups. That is one reason why we are scared of returning with you. We don't know what to expect.

"Zusa, sometimes the stories you tell your audience seem to be full of mystical experiences. That is something that frightens us. For it is said that in our culture, mysticism cannot be expressed in words. In fact, in our language, we do not have an equivalent word for mysticism. Yet somehow you have found a way, without prior knowledge of your topic, of communicating a message to all people in a clear, understandable manner. By all accounts, people have started to believe every word you say, regardless of whether your storytelling is true or false. This is very dangerous and might put every one of us at risk."

It was Motke who spoke up. "Perhaps we should sleep on all that has just been told and talk again tomorrow morning."

Everyone agreed.

13

Oh Motke, what have I done?" said Zusa. "The Klezmers no longer love me. They believe I am a supernatural being, a mystic, they said. I'm not, am I? I don't have special powers. I'm just a storyteller of dreams who willingly communicates my feelings and thoughts to others. I don't interpret my dreams for people. Yes, my dreams feel intense to me, but why would people start believing them, and why are the Klezmers so frightened?"

"Zusa, do you believe in your dreams? Do you believe they are true? You communicate your inner feelings and thoughts to your audience with such authority that they select the pieces of it they want to believe.

"The other day I overheard someone say that they think you are a great optimist, that you have faith and meaning in what you say and that you have a great ability to communicate with others.

"Zusa, believe me, you are not a mystic. I have known you all my life. Unlike many mystics, you are not pessimistic. You believe in life, you have a vision of all people someday being equal, of people without prejudice living together, side-by-side, without hate, and ignorance.

"Some things are hard to figure out. Perhaps during that rainstorm, we should never have entered the forest. Perhaps we should have found shelter elsewhere. Perhaps we are still in the forest as children, and all of this is just a lucid dream."

"For both of us?" said Zusa.

"Yes, for both of us. Do you remember when we were very young, our parents, yours and mine, always told us to stay away from the evil forest? They said the people who lived in it had magical powers. None of Sanok's children ever went near the forest."

Motke smiled gently at Zusa. "And now look at us. We proudly call ourselves The Children of the Forest, and we say that with pride. Yet our Klezmers, our dear, dear friends, who regard us as their family, have become frightened of us. Their experience in our forest cannot be explained. They do not know what happened to them from the time they entered our forest as children to the time they arrived in Skookum as adults. They have no way of knowing or proving what happened to them. You heard what they had to say. They regard us as children they could never have. Yet, we continually share with them our positive experiences and our love for the five righteous forest grown-ups who saved us."

"The Exodus from Egypt occurs in every human being,
in every era, in every year, and in every day."

14

"I have some good news," announced Saul. "We have all been invited to perform at the Skookum Music Festival of the Arts. We leave for Skookum tomorrow."

Motke looked at Zusa. He smiled at her as if to say we are returning to where we started our voyage many years ago. It's the nearest town to our forest. Deldor looked at Zusa; she wasn't smiling.

Remarkably, on their arrival, Skookum looked much the same as the day they first arrived so many years ago. Colourful historic buildings adorned with flowers and flags featured throughout the town. Traditional horse-drawn carriages, with their horses wearing feathered headdresses, waited patiently to be hired.

As Zusa and Motke entered the Town Square they both had a surreal feeling that something wasn't as it should be. It was as if they had stepped back in time. Nothing had changed in the ensuing years since they had first arrived in Skookum as teenagers. The same farmers at their fruit and vegetable stalls and the tradespeople selling their pots and pans hadn't aged at all! Even the clothes they were wearing were the same. And they were all staring at Zusa and Motke in an eerie manner.

Nearby, children were playing a game from another era. They were having fun playing Serso, a game where two children stand in front of each other and quickly toss and catch a round ring onto a stick.

"Where are we?" a startled Motke said to Zusa.

"Come on Motke, it's time to leave this place, right now! I cannot explain what is happening, but I suddenly feel a chill throughout my body. Let's go!"

Eight streets, two to each corner, led away from the Town Square. At one of the corners, Zusa and Motke could see five Klezmers waving, telling them to walk towards their corner.

As they started to walk towards the Klezmers, they were followed silently, step-by-step, in one long line, first by the children and then by the market's merchants. There was a loneliness about them all, as they stared neither to the left nor to the right.

"Motke, do not look back! Keep your eyes fixed on the Klezmers." Zusa tightly held Motke's hand. As they approached their friends, the line behind them separated, divided into two. One by one, some went to the right, but most went to the left. And then, they all vanished.

"By the expression on your faces, you look as if you've seen the souls of dead people," Leah said to Zusa and Motke.

"Yes, it felt as if we had, as soon as we walked into the Town Square," said Motke. Zusa described their experience, leaving not one detail out.

The five Klezmers were astonished as they listened to Zusa's account, for none of them had the slightest idea of what happened.

"We were waving to you to hurry up and join us. We are late for our rehearsal at the Music Centre. Behind you, in the Town Square, from where we were standing, we only saw children happily playing games and the stall owners selling their products," said Daniel.

"Both of you have such a vivid imagination!" laughed Sarah in her musical way of talking.

"It was no imagination!" It was Deldor, who had now joined the rest of the Klezmers. "I also saw what they experienced." All the attention was now directed onto Deldor.

"What do you mean?" asked Saul. "Deldor, what are you saying?"

Tears slowly fell from Deldor's eyes to her cheeks. "Memories, Saul. Memories of the worst kind. Memories we have all been trying to hide from ourselves. Enough! It is time we found out who we are. There are so many pieces missing from our lives that our memories have shielded from us."

Deldor's tearful face looked softly at Zusa and Motke. "I have decided to return with you to your forest."

15

The Skookum Music Centre was a magnificent structure dating back many centuries. It was known for its superb acoustics and beauty with fine murals depicting famous musical artists such as Chopin, Szymanowski, Kurpiński, Deszner, and Luria.

It was here, after Motke and the Klezmers had performed to a standing ovation from the audience, that Zusa made her astonishing speech. With no introduction, she slowly came on stage dressed in a pure white lace dress. Tiny pink and blue ribbons adorned her blond hair. She carried a bouquet containing an assortment of red poppies, lavender, violets, and lotus flowers. Zusa silently looked at the audience for what must have been three minutes, while the audience sat there, in a deathly hush, not knowing what would happen:

"My friends, last evening I had a dream. I will now share it with you."

"I believe our world here is strengthened by righteous people, irrespective of one's rank in society, religion, colour, nationality, or physical appearance. A world that no longer wishes to have the word hate in its vocabulary. A world that no longer wishes to seek revenge for the injustices carried out by previous generations."

Zusa walked slowly to the front of the stage and faced the audience.

"My world should also be your world. In my dream, I attended a meeting given by the great ninth-century Jewish philosopher Saadia Gaon. Learned scholars from many religions and countries were present. Saadia spoke about revenge. He said that the thirst for revenge gives the pleasure of seeing the humiliation of its enemy, appeases the vehemence of its wrath, and puts an end to excessive brooding. Saadia said that people who are consumed by the desire for revenge get into a frame of mind of refusing to accept mediation or entertaining any feeling of compassion or pity or listening to any plea for clemency.

"Is this where we are today? Over nine hundred years later Saadia's comments still vibrate in the attitude that we have learned nothing. And as we continue to observe the hatred and intolerance between us, between those exclaiming a sense of victimhood between our political elites, we find very little is based upon the two-way acceptance that my world is also your world."

Zusa extended her arms outward and beckoned the audience to listen to her. She took a deep breath.

"My friends, this will be the last time I will be speaking publicly. The future is in your hands and in the hands of your children. May you be able to grasp what the future has in store for all of us. I have no more to say. Now, go in peace."

As Zusa walked off the stage, Motke and all six Klezmers, Saul, Anna, Daniel, Leah, Sarah, and Deldor were waiting for her. Each of them, crying, one by one, hugged her.

It was Saul who spoke. "Zusa, collectively we have decided. We all will be joining you and Motke at your wedding, in your forest."

Zusa gazed at Deldor. Deldor smiled and nodded in agreement.

The next few days were full of laughter, planning, and love. No one worried about the unknown. For this was the time not to look back at the past, but to look forward to hearing again about the five righteous forest grown-ups Zusa and Motke had met many years ago.

"Please tell us once more of their mystical powers and the compassion they showed you," said Anna.

Zusa and Motke repeatedly took turns telling the

Klezmers about their journey from the time they entered the forest to their arrival in Skookum.

They told the stories of Hanka, who could not smell or taste; of Danek, who had no hearing; of Zavel, the blind man; of Lejka, the young woman in the wheelchair and of Sura, the stutterer who found comfort in singing. Their stories always ended by saying they are living proof of being able to enter and exit the forest of no beginning and no end.

Yet, the Klezmers remained hesitant about what would happen to them if the forest didn't willingly accept their return. For as Daniel said, unlike Zusa and Motke, they had no memory of their time there.

Zusa took Daniel's hand. "Yes, I understand how wary you must be. Believe in us Daniel, for before we all return to our forest every one of you must resolve your uncertainties and doubts and have an open mind. Will you be able to do that?"

16

The day finally arrived. The Klezmers packed their musical instruments, Saul, his trumpet; Leah, her violin; Daniel, his straw harmonica and clarinet; Anna, her hammered dulcimer; Sarah, her flute; and Deldor, her accordion. By late morning, they were on the road leading to the forest.

It is said that time cannot be cured. For very little had changed since Zusa and Motke made their original journey so many years ago from their forest to Skookum. And now, they were returning to where it all began.

As they walked along the dusty road, they observed the farm carts and horses and sparsely populated villages, abandoned wooden houses, older women wearing traditional floral headscarves while carrying pails of water from the village pump, and the ever-standing church and graveyard, weary from its long history. Very little had changed. As they passed, no villager offered to speak to them or even give them a nod of their head in acknowledgment.

Towards the forest, their shadows slowly faded, the warm sun on their backs had almost disappeared, and the blue sky in front of them had taken on the appearance of an impending storm.

Yet, it didn't rain. It was as if a painter had drawn a line across the sky. On one side, the sun was behind them. On the opposing side, the dark clouds in the forest continued to be more menacing at every step of the way.

They reached the edge of the forest by late afternoon. Facing them were huge trees measuring over 35 metres in height, including Beech, Black Poplar, Larch, and Silver Fir. All looked formidable and intent on blocking their entrance.

"Look over there, there's a gap!" Motke pointed to a place where an amber glow emanated from between two dead pine tree trunks. "It's starting to rain. Come on! The forest will shelter us."

"No!" screamed Deldor. "Not there!" She looked towards the amber glow. "There is a spark of darkness emerging from it. I am not entering the forest from there. Those dead tree trunks, they were once the Tree of Life and the Tree of Knowledge, of humanity itself."

The Klezmers hesitated. It was Daniel who stepped forward. He turned towards his Klezmer friends. "Do you remember what Zusa said to me? She said before we all return to the forest every one of us must resolve our uncertainties and doubts and have an open mind."

He turned towards Deldor and held her hand. "We cannot enter the forest without you. Have faith in Zusa and Motke. If you have any fears or suspicions, remove them now. Our journey will not be brought to completion without you."

Motke gently smiled. "It is time. Nightfall is approaching. We must go. As we enter the forest and continue our journey, do not look back at where we came from, or place one foot off the path." Deldor glanced at her Klezmer friends, embraced Daniel, and nodded her head in agreement. Zusa and Motke each took Deldor's hands and whispered to her, "We'll protect you. For you have nothing to fear from us, or from our forest."

All the Klezmers acquiesced and nervously entered the forest with Zusa and Motke leading the way.

“Where there is no compassion, crime increases.”

-Part Three-

17

The forest was not what the Klezmers had at all expected, or as it was told in stories and fables many years later. This forest beckoned them in, showing the way through Zusa and Motke. The branches of the trees seem to open a solitary path further into the woodland. No rain had found its way into the forest or onto the path, which was of a rich golden-brown colour, for it was dry and contained no footprints of earlier travellers, only those of the Klezmers. If the Klezmers had dared to look back at where they had come from, they would not have found their footprints. They had mystically disappeared.

Zusa assured the Klezmers that if they remained on the path and did not look back, she would be with them day and night. "My friends, I had a dream to use my skills to make sure you are not harmed." She paused and looked directly at Deldor, "as long as you all do everything I request." Deldor trembled!

It was Saul, the leader of the Klezmers, who spoke up. "Zusa, we are prepared for whatever you may command of us. For you have shown us your skills in leading us to this place. For sure, you and Motke are The Children of the Forest."

Later that night, after eating a simple meal prepared in advance by Anna, consisting of cold borscht, cabbage, and noodles, and for dessert, Sernick, a traditional cheesecake, the Klezmers bedded down amongst the bushes, which had produced a soft blanket of feathers for them to sleep on. As the Klezmers gradually fell asleep, in the distance they could hear a voice singing a sweet lullaby they remembered from their childhood days. *Kotki dwa* (Two kittens).

Zusa smiled at the Klezmers. "Ah! That must be Sura's voice!"

> *Aaa, kotki dwa, szarobure obydwa, nic nie będą robiły, tylko ciebie bawiły.*
>
> *Ah, two kittens, both mottled grey, they won't do anything but entertain you.*

Silent tears flowed unashamedly from Sarah as

she recalled the fond memories of her loving parents singing the lullaby to her baby sister, the day before her mother, father and sister were taken away, while she hid under the bed.

Morning came. Motke awoke to see Zusa smiling over him. "Motke, come, while the Klezmers sleep, let's go for a walk."

Zusa held his arm and put her head on his shoulder. "We are kindred spirits. You know, over the years you have continued to support me at every corner, at every adventure of my life. You have become my vanguard. Your quiet, determined manner has brought peace to me. I know our future lives, together in marriage, will bring us great joy."

"But?" said Motke.

"But I am frightened. I am terrified of my dreams becoming reality. It is as if I hear a voice in my dreams from behind a wall giving me commands, and therefore I must assume the realness of that human being since a human voice can originate only from another existing human being. That wall, Motke, is getting larger with every day we take in the forest, our forest. Do I make myself clear to you? I am so confused."

Motke gently stroked Zusa's blonde hair and looked into her blue eyes. "Zusa, we all have doubts about ourselves, about our abilities. There's an ancient story of sailors who were sunk in seas of doubt. They were overcome by waves of confusion. Sadly, there was no diver to bring them up from the depths, nor a swimmer who might take hold of their hands and bring them ashore. My dear Zusa, I have been tasked to bring you ashore so that you may continue your journey, wherever it personally leads you."

"And you? remarked Zusa. "Will you be joining me?"

"Yes, yes!" Motke hesitated. "Yes, of course."

The two walked back, hand-in-hand, to where the Klezmers slept.

"Where is Sarah?" Other than Leah, none of the Klezmers could offer any important information as to where Sarah had disappeared. Leah did recollect Sarah becoming emotional at hearing a voice singing from somewhere deep in the forest, the direction from which they had come.

"Perhaps Sarah went back to find the singer," said Anna to Zusa.

Zusa's voice showed her frustration with the Klezmers. "Don't you remember my words to all of you? I told you not to look back at where we had come from or attempt to retrace our previous steps.

"Within this forest are powerful nature spirits that go beyond anything you can ever imagine. They not only look after the trees, plants, and animals, but also are accountable for the weather. They are the protectors of all that surrounds you. But they will not protect you or your shadow. So, my friends, listen to my every word and do everything I say.

"You are good people, but in your present form,

you are all naïve to the understanding of our forest."

Zusa looked at Deldor. "Deldor, never forget what Motke and I whispered to you. Do you remember?" Deldor nodded in agreement. "Yes, you whispered, 'we'll protect you. For you have nothing to fear from us or our forest.'"

Zusa turned towards the Klezmers. "You are correct. I did say that! But I can only protect each of you if you follow my commands."

Saul approached Zusa. "Tell us, where we are? For as we know it, it feels like it is neither the future nor past nor present."

Motke put his hands on Saul's shoulders. "Saul, I believe it is only a blind man such as yourself that would reach out to ask such a question. I believe it is you, a blind man, who can see far more than any of us. Our forest, which we have named The Children of the Forest, cries out to be released from the burden it has had to bear for so long. For here, children have found shelter from the ravages of hate, discrimination, and conflict. Every child has the right to be alive; every child deserves equal treatment. Remember, for here, where you stand, time does not exist, at least, not as you know it outside the forest."

"And Sarah? What has happened to her?" said Anna.

"In all truthfulness, at this time, I do not know. The nature spirits surrounding us are mischievous entities."

It was Daniel who spoke up. "Zusa, Motke, we are in your hands. We are simple people. You are responsible for us, as we were for you during your early innocent years in Skookum. But now, we are an old and weary group of Klezmers. Help us to understand what mystical beings exist here in your forest. Zusa, give us a small clue that we can grasp onto so that we will have the courage to face the days ahead."

Zusa responded: "I cannot give you what you ask. But I will ask you to continue living your daily lives here with the gentleness and feelings you had for each other during your younger Klezmer days. And now, if you are ready, we should move on."

The second day began uneventfully. The path wound its way deeper into the forest, through clumps of Prickly Ash, Beaked Hazelnut, and Bladdernut, while branches of the trees knelt to protect their visitors from the deadly Castor Bean and Hogweed plants.

As they silently walked, Sarah was on everyone's mind, fearful they would never see her again, as well as being unsure of their own future.

The Klezmers took turns pushing Leah's wheelchair. Motke followed up behind them, while Zusa, a few steps ahead, watched for any obstacles that might impede their journey.

"What is that delightful smell?" Leah asked Zusa. "Can it be Golabki? Impossible! Here in the forest? Cabbage leaves, stuffed with ground beef and rice?"

Some metres ahead, on the side of the path, a table had been laid for them with Golabki, sour cream, and mashed potatoes, and for dessert, rugelach, filled with strawberries and apples.

Zusa looked at Motke. Silently, they smiled at each other, for they remembered as children their meeting with Lejka, the forest wheelchair acrobat. She had given them identical food to take with them for their onward forest journey.

"How could this be?" said Leah. "I'm hungry. Shall we eat?"

"And it shall be as when a hungry man dreameth, and behold, he eateth, but he awaketh, and his soul is empty... Isaiah 29:8. I'm sorry. I don't know how I came to utter such words," said Saul. "I opened my mouth and the words just seemed to originate from another place."

Deldor stepped forward. Her hands were shaking. "It is a message for us, an omen. It is like that of an anxious person who has a pleasant dream, only to awake to find it is not true." She turned towards Zusa. "The more we travel into the forest, the more we must listen and obey every word spoken by Zusa. We must trust her with our lives."

The meal was a great success and although the disappearance of Sarah continued to be on everyone's mind, the food, for the most part, helped to placate the fears of what might lie ahead for the Klezmers.

After they were all bedded down for the night, amongst a soft blanket of feathers, it was Leah whose words startled Zusa and Motke.

"May you be able to lie down in peace at night and return to life the following day."

These were the exact words used by the righteous

forest grown-ups to Zusa and Motke.

And again, during the darkest period of the night, while Anna, Daniel, Deldor, and Saul slept, it was Leah who alarmed Zusa and Motke.

"Just look at what I can do," Leah remarked as she performed the same wheelie stunt while sitting in her wheelchair that had been performed by Leika many years ago. They included balancing herself on the wheelchair's two back wheels, and spinning on one wheel around, so much so that Leah not only became dizzy, but her conduct caused her to fall into unconsciousness.

None of the other Klezmers awoke to become aware of the events that took place. For the forest's nature spirits had wrapped them in a dusting of lavender oil for the duration of the night.

Day three arrived. The number three had always been significant for Deldor. She defined it as one of the 'perfect numbers.'

"Always remember," she would explain to her Klezmer colleagues, "in our sacred writings the number three implies excellence. The number three always identifies some important event leading to our destiny."

That destiny was far beyond the imagination of the Klezmers, although for Zusa and Motke, their hopes and goals were focused on their forest marriage and thereafter returning to Sanok to find out what had happened to their parents.

As on the day previous, Zusa took the lead by walking ahead of the Klezmers, while Motke, for the most part, walked at the rear. He occasionally helped Anna, Saul, and Daniel, taking turns wheeling Leah, who remained unconscious.

Anna approached Zusa. "Do you mind if I ask you a question?" Zusa acknowledged Anna with a nod of her head but did not distract her eyes from the path ahead.

"What is it that you expect from me?" replied Zusa. There was no warmth in her voice towards Anna, as there had been before they entered the forest.

"I'm sorry, Zusa, I should not have disturbed you, but since entering the forest I have been hearing voices. They started as voices of elderly people, and as you've gradually led us deeper into the forest, the voices have become younger."

"And now?" responded Zusa.

"They have become voices of my childhood, of children laughing and playing together. They have become more dominant. The children's voices are familiar to me."

"Familiar in what way?"

"Of my late brothers, sisters, and cousins, asking me why I did not join them. The voices deride me for living. Zusa, I am afraid of hearing these voices; I'm afraid of myself. Can you help me?"

"Anna, is there something else you want to tell me about your voices?"

"Well, each voice I hear also conveys a colour."

"Can you be more specific?"

"When I hear the voices of elderly people I am

surrounded by a sensation of dark colours, such as black and grey. And I am disheartened. Yet, with the children's voices, I am aroused by a feeling of warm colours, such as red and yellow."

"And what else?"

"At last evening's dinner, I could neither smell nor taste the food."

It was Anna's last comment that brought Zusa to a halt. She turned towards the other Klezmers and gestured for Motke to join her. "Let us rest here for a while."

"Motke, do you remember the righteous forest grown-up we met during our first day in this forest? She couldn't smell or taste the food. And we asked her how it was possible she could make such a wonderful meal for us if she couldn't smell or have a taste for the food."

Motke smiled. "Yes, I think I remember now. Wasn't her name Hanka? She explained it by showing us how the colours of different foods growing in the forest encouraged her to produce a delicious meal."

Zusa was not smiling. She repeated the conversation she had had with Anna. "Motke, the deeper we walk into this forest... it is as if everything has been decided for us beforehand. What are we doing to our dear friends? Why did we persuade the Klezmers to come with us? Is our future to be repeated? Perhaps it was wrong to bring them here."

Motke put his arm around Zusa's shoulder. "You talk as if it is fate. Knowing our history and that of the Klezmers, are you saying we have come into this world to continue living our lives without change, and to accept what has happened will recur?"

"Zusa, since when have you been a pessimist? What we have achieved together so far has been truly amazing. You have been our captain, our leader. Even now, the fact that you are walking ahead of us, and I am in the rear, shows us all your authority. Zusa, we are on a path, accompanied by our friends, that will result in our marriage."

"Yes, Motke, thank you for those kind words. But what of Sarah? What of Leah? And now what is to happen with Anna? As a leader, I have failed."

"Zusa, look at me. You are our leader, and you have not failed. I promise you that! But now, we should move on. It is getting late, and darkness will soon be upon us."

"Who lacks confidence speaks lies more readily."

18

Day four. Sarah had still not reappeared. Leah had not woken up, and Anna continued to complain about hearing children's voices and being unable to smell or taste food.

Zusa invited Saul to join her up front, while Motke and Deldor wheeled Leah in the rear and Anna preferred to remain in the middle of the group by herself.

Saul held on to Zusa's arm as they walked in silence. But it was far from being compatible.

"What troubles you, Zusa?"

"How did you know that I ...?"

A warm chuckle came from Saul.

"Zusa, I have been blind from birth. Yet, like you I can socialize, I can tell the difference between day and night by hearing the sounds surrounding me, such as your breathing. It is as if I have an invisible teacher, instructing me on the ways of the forest. When I step on a fallen twig from a tree or bush, I know from the sound what season it is. From touching the forest flowers, I know from the smell the differences in the fragrance and beauty you can see in each variety. And now I can hear in your silence that you are distressed."

Saul put his hand on Zusa's arm. "Why are you crying, dear Zusa?"

"I am crying out of fear. The words you have just shared with me are the same words said by Zavel, the blind man, in this forest many years ago when we were children. Are you the same Zavel we met? And is it the same for your friends, Anna, who reminds us of Hanka and Leah, who acts in the same way as Lejka, and of Sarah, who also sang and stuttered as did Sura in this forest? Saul, I need to arrive at the truth!"

"Ah, Zusa! It has been said that some are presented with the truth yet are in doubt about it."

"Saul, I will not doubt your integrity."

"And yet, my dear Zusa, you, our storyteller of dreams, sometimes offering the truth is an act that gives pleasure to the giver, but might inflict grief on the receiver. I cannot live in your world knowing I have given you sorrow. Now, wipe away your tears before they turn into torrents of water. Tomorrow will be the fifth day in your forest. Your wedding day. We will have reached the end of this path."

Night came quickly to all those present. The forest's trees and plants were quieter than usual. The nature spirits, all too willing in the past to show their mischievous behaviour, were silent. A dark cloud in the air infiltrated all those present as if they were witnessing a change. And the moon, since it does not have its own light, grasped futilely to just reflect a mere morsel of sunlight.

It was Deldor and her accordion, with her musical intonation, who helped to arouse the souls surrounding her from their bleakness. She was joined by Daniel on his clarinet, Anna on her hammered dulcimer, and Saul on his trumpet which the blending of these harmonious melodies awoke Leah and her violin from their deep sleep.

Whatever melancholy atmosphere pervaded the forest previously that night, the combined musical efforts of those present, coupled with the sudden appearance of Sarah brought them together again for tomorrow's wedding celebration.

"Where there is no peace, prayers are not heard."

19

During the night and into the early morning of day five, Zusa experienced a dream of such magnitude that it went far beyond what she had ever previously experienced. And for the first time, Motke, her beloved, and the Klezmers would not be permitted to share in its content.

Zusa awoke to find the number 36 had been heavily scorched on the forest floor next to her, where she had slept. This same number had featured prominently in her dream. In addition, a silver amulet had been placed around her neck.

None of the Klezmers accepted ownership of the amulet or the scorched earth, and among themselves, they evaded talking about it. However, Deldor did not! She approached Zusa and wanted to know if she could comfort her. Zusa readily agreed.

Motke, for once, did not express support for Zusa. For he too had experienced a dream, but he had no difficulty sharing it with Saul, Anna, Daniel, Sarah, and Leah.

“Last night I dreamed of being on a path. I was alone. The path had a sign directing me to walk east. It said, The Path of Righteousness. Along the way, I passed many people who were lined up, as if to greet me. When I passed they asked me to bless them, and when I said I was not skilled in the practice, they wept. I could not look them in the eye.”

The Klezmers listened to Motke’s story as they encircled him with great interest and surrounded him in support, except for Deldor

“Suddenly, I recognized two voices. I turned to see the images of my dear mother and father, my mamme and my tate. Their images were the same as I remembered them, all those years ago. They were smiling and gestured for me to join them in walking together along the path.

I asked my father, “Where am I? Why are you here at this moment?” He replied, “We are here to help you along this path. It is a continuing journey for you, leading you to be a great, compassionate leader of your future nation-state that exudes trust and honesty.”

I responded, “But tomorrow I am getting

married. Is this not the same path I have taken for the past four days with Zusa and my Klezmer friends?

"My mother looked at me, shook her head, and said: No, my dear Motke. It is not. This path is for you alone to determine your future. And you must select which path of the two you intend to take. With those words, my parents disappeared!"

Nothing was further from Zusa's mind that afternoon than the dream of preparing for her wedding.

As Zusa, Motke and the Klezmers walked towards the end of the forest path, a vast cave appeared in front of them, big enough to hold every honest person from the many towns and villages they had visited years ago.

Gradually, as if by some mystical power, the righteous forest grown-ups from Zusa's and Motke's past, Hanka, Danek, Zavel, Lejka, and Sura, appeared at intervals according to the order in which they originally appeared. And they, simultaneously by the power of miracles, used the wind and their breath to transport all the Klezmer groups in the land to this site.

To adorn the entrance of the cave, they gathered many glorious, coloured leaves and a plethora of forest flowers, which started to glow and blaze brightly to form a multitude of bright lights of different tints and tones.

One righteous soul stepped forward and asked all those present to join hands, form a circle, close their eyes, and pray to bring Zusa and Motke together.

Other than Deldor, her Klezmer friends were

nowhere to be seen.

All those present embraced, while Zusa, alone, trembling at the cave's entrance, waited hopefully for Motke to appear.

ABOUT THE AUTHOR

Alan L. Simons is a British-born Canadian author, writer and social & allyship advocate. As a diplomat, he served as the Honorary Consul of the Republic of Rwanda to Canada in the post-genocide era. He lectures and writes on issues relating to religion in politics, antisemitism, intolerance, hate, Islamofascism, conflict and terrorism.

ALSO BY ALAN L. SIMONS

EIGHTEEN MONTHS-A LOVE STORY INTERRUPTED

A story of a human relationship that testifies to the strength and will of both the terminally ill patient and her partner as he comes to accept her illness and the brief period they will spend together.

THE VILLAGE OF LITTLE COMELY-ON-THE-MARSH

This hilarious and satirical story is about the lives of an eccentric Welsh community living in a small village somewhere in southeastern France, exclusively in their own sheltered world.

THE VILLAGE OF LITTLE PLETZL-ON-THE-ZUMP

The Village of Little Pletzl-on-the-Zump weaves around the lives of a bizarre Yiddish-speaking community of 613 people living for hundreds of years in a small village also in southeastern France. They speak a unique dialect called Frantsoydish.

THE VILLAGE OF LITTLE FIGGY-ON-THE-DUFF

The Village of Little Figgy-on-the-Duff, the final book in the Village Trilogy, is an eclectic and wonderfully engaging story about what happens to an eccentric and homogeneous community of Newfoundlanders and Labradorians, whose ancestors originally fled their homeland because of a fear that the Vikings would make them wear traditional Norse clothing and take over the dry salt cod industry.

AN ANTHOLOGY OF WITTY & ODDBALL VILLAGE STORIES

Village Stories for Like-Minded Friends. Many years ago, three distinct communities, from Newfoundland and Labrador, Wales, and Eastern Europe, each found their way to southeastern France, where they happily established themselves exclusively in their own concealed worlds, without a care or a familiarity with their surroundings. That is, until a stranger of senior years had the tenacity to venture forth on a path to document more of what had been little written about them. I acknowledge to you from the outset that I am that stranger.

FOR CHILDREN

THE INCREDIBLE ADVENTURES OF CAPTAIN MACDUDDYFUNK IN CUGGERMUGGERLAND

The children of Canada's Minister of Missing Islands are magically transported to the mysterious island of Cuggermuggerland, where they meet the Quidnuncs, who love to hug, and the Shilpits, who always scream and shout at each other. Captain MacDuddyfunk escorts the two children through a series of exciting adventures, culminating in Allison and Richard showing the Quidnuncs and the Shilpits that two diverse communities can come together to live in harmony.

SWEATY CATS AND BABY PIGEONS

Eight short stories are written for the inquiring mind of a young child, with the view that grandparents play an important role in the development of their little loved ones. Many grandparents have had to accept that their grandchildren do not live around the corner from them. Therefore, intensive periods of involvement with them are relatively short. Yet, we still strive at every opportunity to keep in touch with our grandchildren.

“Disparage no book, for it is also part of the world.”

https://thechildrenoftheforest.com

thechildrenoftheforest@proton.me

https://alanlsimons.com

www.ingramcontent.com/pod-product-compliance
Lightning Source LLC
La Vergne TN
LVHW091007080826
845145LV00003B/1162

* 9 7 8 1 7 7 8 2 1 3 7 8 6 *